First published in *The Adventures of Mr Toad* 1998
by Walker Books Ltd, 87 Vauxhall Walk, London SE11 5HJ

This edition produced 2004 for
The Book People Ltd, Hall Wood Avenue,
Haydock, St Helens WA11 9UL

2 4 6 8 10 9 7 5 3 1

This book has been typeset in Bembo

Printed in China

British Library Cataloguing in Publication Data:
a catalogue record for this book is available from the British Library

ISBN 1-84428-975-3

www.walkerbooks.co.uk

Toad's Adventures

from
The Wind in the Willows

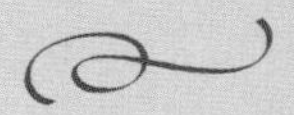

Written by
KENNETH GRAHAME

Abridged and illustrated by
INGA MOORE

TED SMART

Toad's Adventures

When Toad found himself in a dungeon, and knew that all the grim darkness of a medieval fortress lay between him and the world of sunshine and high roads where he had lately been so happy, he flung himself at full length on the floor, and shed bitter tears. "This is the end of everything," he said, "at least it is the end of Toad, which is the same thing. O unhappy and forsaken Toad!" He passed his days and nights for several weeks, refusing his meals or intermediate light refreshments, though the gaoler, knowing Toad's pockets were well lined, frequently pointed out that many comforts, indeed luxuries, could be sent in – at a price – from the outside.

Now the gaoler had a daughter. This kind-hearted girl said to her father one day, "I can't bear to see that poor beast so unhappy and getting so thin! You let me have the managing of him. I'll make him eat."

Her father replied that she could do what she liked with him. He was tired of Toad and his sulks. So she went and knocked on the door of Toad's cell.

"Cheer up, Toad," she said, entering. "Sit up and try a bit of dinner. See, I've brought you some of mine, hot from the oven!" It was bubble-and-squeak, between two plates, and its fragrance filled the narrow cell. The penetrating smell of cabbage reached the nose of Toad as he lay prostrate in his misery on the floor, and gave him the idea for a moment that life was not such a desperate thing as he had imagined. But still he wailed, and kicked his legs, and refused to be comforted. So the wise girl retired, but, of course, the smell of hot cabbage remained, as it will do, and Toad, between sobs, sniffed and reflected and gradually began to think new thoughts; of chivalry and poetry, and deeds still to be done; of meadows, and cattle browsing in them; kitchen-gardens, and straight herb-borders, and warm snap-dragon beset by bees. The air of the cell took on a rosy tinge: he began to think of his friends, and how they would surely be able to do something; of lawyers, and what an ass he had been not to get a few; and lastly, he thought of his own cleverness and resource, and all that he was capable of if he only gave his great mind to it; and the cure was almost complete.

When the girl returned, some hours later, she carried a tray, with a cup of tea steaming on it; and a plate piled up with hot buttered toast. The smell of that toast simply talked to Toad; talked of warm kitchens; breakfast on bright frosty mornings, cosy firesides on winter evenings, when one's ramble was over and slippered feet were propped on the fender. Toad sat up, dried his eyes, sipped his tea and munched his toast, and soon began talking freely about himself, and the house he lived in, his doings there, and what a lot his friends thought of him.

The gaoler's daughter encouraged him to go on.

"Tell me about Toad Hall," she said. "It sounds beautiful. But first wait till I fetch you some more tea and toast."

She tripped away, and returned with a fresh trayful; and Toad, pitching in, told her about the boathouse, the fish-pond and the old walled kitchen-garden; about the pig-sties and the stables, the pigeon-house, and the hen-house; and about the dairy and the wash-house, the china cupboards, and the linen-presses (she liked that bit especially); about the banqueting hall, and the fun they had there when the other animals were gathered round the table and Toad was at his best, singing songs, telling stories, carrying on generally. Then she wanted to know about his friends, and was very interested in all he had to tell her about them and how they were, and what they did to pass their time. When she said good night, having filled his water-jug and shaken up his straw for him, Toad curled himself up and had an excellent night's rest and the pleasantest of dreams.

They had many interesting talks together as the dreary days went on; and the gaoler's daughter grew very sorry for Toad, and thought it a shame that a poor animal should be locked up in prison for what seemed to her a trivial offence.

One morning she said, "Toad, listen. I have an aunt who is a washerwoman."

"Never mind," said Toad affably. "*I* have several aunts who *ought* to be washerwomen."

"Do be quiet, Toad," said the girl. "As I said, I have an aunt; she does the washing for the prisoners in this castle. Now, she's very poor. A few pounds would mean a lot to her. If you could come to some arrangement by which she would let you have her dress and bonnet, you could escape from the castle as the official washerwoman. You're very alike in many respects – particularly about the figure."

"We're *not*," said Toad. "I have a very elegant figure – for what I am."

"So has my aunt," replied the girl, "for what *she* is. But have it your own way. You horrid, proud, ungrateful animal, when I'm sorry for you, and trying to help you!"

"Yes, yes, thank you very much indeed," said Toad. "But look here! you wouldn't surely have Toad, of Toad Hall, going about the country disguised as a washerwoman!"

"Then you can stop here as Toad," replied the girl.

Toad was always ready to admit himself in the wrong. "You are a good, kind, clever girl," he said, "and I am a stupid toad. Introduce me to your worthy aunt, if you will be so kind."

Next evening the girl ushered her aunt into Toad's cell, bearing his week's washing pinned up in a towel. The sight of certain gold sovereigns thoughtfully placed on the table left little to discuss. In return for his cash, Toad received a cotton print gown, an apron, a shawl and a rusty black bonnet; the only stipulation the old lady made being that she should be gagged and bound and dumped in a corner.

"Now, Toad," said the girl. "Take off that coat and waistcoat of yours; you're fat enough as it is."

Shaking with laughter, she proceeded to "hook-and-eye" him into the gown, arranged the shawl with a professional fold, and tied the bonnet under his chin.

"You're the very image of her," she giggled, "only I'm sure you never looked so respectable in all your life. Now, good-bye, Toad, and good luck. Go straight down the way you came up; and if anyone says anything to you, as they probably will, being men, you can chaff back a bit, of course, but remember you're a widow woman, with a character to lose."

With a quaking heart, Toad set forth on what seemed to be a hare-brained and hazardous undertaking; but he was soon surprised to find how easy everything was made for him. The washerwoman's squat figure in its familiar cotton print seemed a passport for every barred door and grim gateway; even when he hesitated, uncertain as to the right turning to take, he found himself helped by the warder at the next gate, anxious to be off to his tea, summoning him to come along sharp and not keep him waiting all night.

At last he heard
the wicket-gate in the
great outer door click behind
him, felt the air of the outer world
upon his brow, and knew that he was free!

Dizzy with the easy success of his daring exploit, he walked quickly towards the town. As he walked along, his attention was caught by some red and green lights a little way off, and the sound of puffing and snorting of engines fell on his ear. "Aha!" he thought, "this is a piece of luck! A railway-station."

He made his way to the station, consulted a time-table, and found that a train, bound more or less in the direction of home, was due to start in half an hour. "More luck!" said Toad, and went off to the booking-office to buy his ticket.

He gave the name of the station nearest Toad Hall, and put his fingers where his waistcoat pocket should have been and found – not only no money, but no pocket to hold it, and no waistcoat to hold the pocket!

To his horror he recollected that he had left both coat and waistcoat behind him in his cell, and with them his money, keys, matches, watch, pencil-case – all that makes life worth living. He made one desperate effort to carry the thing off, and, in his fine old manner he said, "Look here! I find I've left my purse behind. Just give me that ticket, will you, and I'll send the money on tomorrow. I'm well known in these parts."

The clerk stared at him and the rusty black bonnet. "I should think you were well known," he said, "if you've tried this game often. Stand away from the window, madam; you're obstructing the other passengers!"

Baffled and full of despair, he wandered down the platform where the train was standing and tears trickled down his nose.

RAILWAY STATION
PLATFORMS
5 & 6

"Hullo, mother!" said the engine-driver, "what's the trouble?

You don't look particularly cheerful!"

"O, sir!" said Toad, "I am a poor unhappy washerwoman, and I've lost all my money, and can't pay for a ticket, and I *must* get home tonight somehow, and whatever I am to do I don't know. O dear, o dear!"

"That's a bad business," said the engine-driver. "Lost your money – and can't get home – and got some kids, too, waiting for you, I dare say?"

"Any amount," sobbed Toad. "And they'll be hungry – and playing with matches – and upsetting lamps – and quarrelling. O dear, O dear!"

"I'll tell you what," said the good engine-driver. "You're a washerwoman. And I'm an engine-driver and there's no denying it's terribly dirty work. If you'll wash a few shirts for me when you get home, and send 'em along, I'll give you a ride on my engine. It's against the Company's regulations, but we're not so particular in these out-of-the-way parts."

Toad scrambled up into the cab of the engine. Of course, he had never washed a shirt in his life, and couldn't if he tried; but he thought: "When I get home to Toad Hall, and have money again, and pockets to put it in, I will send the engine-driver enough to pay for quite a quantity of washing, and that will be the same thing, or better."

The guard waved his welcome flag, the engine-driver whistled in cheerful response, and the train moved out of the station. As the speed increased, and Toad could see fields, and hedges, and cows, and horses, all flying past him, and as he thought how every minute was bringing him nearer to Toad Hall and friends, and money to chink in his pocket, and a soft bed to sleep in, and good things to eat, and praise and admiration of his adventures and his cleverness, he began to skip up and down and sing snatches of song, to the great astonishment of the engine-driver, who had come across washerwomen before, but never one like this.

They had covered many a mile, and Toad was considering what he would have for supper, when he noticed the engine-driver, with a puzzled expression on his face, was leaning over the side of the engine, listening hard. "It's strange," he said, "we're the last train running tonight, yet I could be sworn I heard another following us."

A dull pain in the lower part of Toad's spine made him want to sit down and try not to think of all the possibilities.

By this time the moon was shining brightly, and presently the engine-driver called out, "I can see it now! It's an engine. It looks as if we're being pursued."

The miserable Toad, crouching in the coal-dust, tried hard to think of something to do, with dismal want of success.

"They are gaining on us fast!" cried the engine-driver. "And the engine is crowded with the queerest lot of people! Warders and policemen all waving and shouting the same thing –

"Stop, stop, stop!"

Toad fell on his knees and cried, "Save me, save me, Mr Engine-driver, I am not the washerwoman I seem to be! I am a toad; and I have just escaped from a loathsome dungeon; and if those fellows on that engine recapture me, it will be chains and bread-and-water misery once more."

The engine-driver looked down on him very sternly, and said, "Now tell the truth; what were you put in prison for?"

"It was nothing much," said Toad, colouring deeply. "I only borrowed a motor-car. I didn't mean to steal it, really."

The engine-driver looked very grave and said, "By rights I ought to give you up. But I don't hold with motor-cars, and I don't hold with being ordered about on my own engine. So cheer up, Toad! I'll do my best, and we may beat them yet!"

They piled on more coals, shovelling furiously; the furnace roared, the sparks flew, the engine leapt and swung, but still their pursuers gained. The engine-driver wiped his brow and said, "It's no good, Toad. They are running light and have the better engine. There's just one thing left to do, it's your only chance, so be ready to jump when I tell you."

The train shot into a tunnel, and the engine roared and rattled, till they shot out at the other end. The driver shut off steam and braked, and as the train slowed down he called, "Now, jump!"

Toad jumped, rolled down a short embankment, picked himself up unhurt, scrambled into a wood and hid.

Peeping out, he saw his train get up speed and disappear at a great pace. Then out of the tunnel burst the pursuing engine, roaring and whistling, her motley crew waving and shouting, "Stop! stop! stop!" When they were past, Toad had a hearty laugh – for the first time since he was thrown into prison.

But he soon stopped when he came to consider that it was now very late and dark and cold, and he was in an unknown wood, with no money and no supper, and still far from friends and home; and the dead silence of everything, after the roar and rattle of the train, was something of a shock.

An owl, swooping towards him, brushed his shoulder with its wing, making him jump. Once he met a fox, who stopped, looked him up and down in a sarcastic sort of way, and said, "Hullo, washerwoman! Half a pair of socks and a pillow-case short this week! Mind it doesn't occur again!" and swaggered off, sniggering. At last he sought the shelter of a hollow tree, where he made himself as comfortable a bed as he could and slept soundly till morning.